ANDY GRIFFITHS

THE 130-STOREY TREEHOUSE

BY

ANDY GRIFFITHS

& TERRY DENTON

MACMILLAN CHILDREN'S BOOKS

First published 2020 by Pan Macmillan Australia Pty Limited
First published in the UK 2020 by Macmillan Children's Books

This paperback edition published 2021 by Macmillan Children's Books
an imprint of Pan Macmillan
The Smithson, 6 Briset Street, London EC1M 5NR
EU representative: Macmillan Publishers Ireland Limited,
Mallard Lodge, Lansdowne Village, Dublin 4
Associated companies throughout the world
www.panmacmillan.com

ISBN 978-1-5290-4593-2

Text copyright © Flying Beetroot Pty Ltd 2020
Illustrations copyright © Terry Denton 2020

The right of Andy Griffiths and Terry Denton to be identified as the
author and illustrator of this work has been asserted by them in
accordance with the Copyright, Designs and Patents Act 1988.

3 5 7 9 8 6 4 2

A CIP catalogue record for this book is available from the British Library.

Typeset in 14/18 Minion Pro by Seymour Designs
Printed and bound by CPI Group (UK) Ltd, Croydon CR0 4YY

The bookshop on pages 24–25 is inspired by a design by Patrick Cookson,
winner of the Readings Bookshop 'Draw Your Dream Bookshop' competition.

THE 130-STOREY TREEHOUSE

Andy Griffiths lives in a 130-storey treehouse with his friend Terry and together they make funny books, just like the one you're holding in your hands right now. Andy writes the words and Terry draws the pictures. If you'd like to know more, read this book (or visit www.andygriffiths.com.au).

Terry Denton lives in a 130-storey treehouse with his friend Andy and together they make funny books, just like the one you're holding in your hands right now. Terry draws the pictures and Andy writes the words. If you'd like to know more, read this book (or visit www.terrydenton.com.au).

CONTENTS

CHAPTER 1

THE 130-STOREY TREEHOUSE

Hi, my name is Andy.

This is my friend Terry.

We live in a tree.

Well, when I say 'tree', I mean treehouse.
And when I say 'treehouse', I don't just mean
any old treehouse—I mean a 130-*storey* treehouse.
(It used to be a 117-storey treehouse, but we've
added another 13 storeys.)

BUZZ!

So what are you waiting for?
Come on up!

6

We've got a soap bubble blaster,

a non-stop dot level,

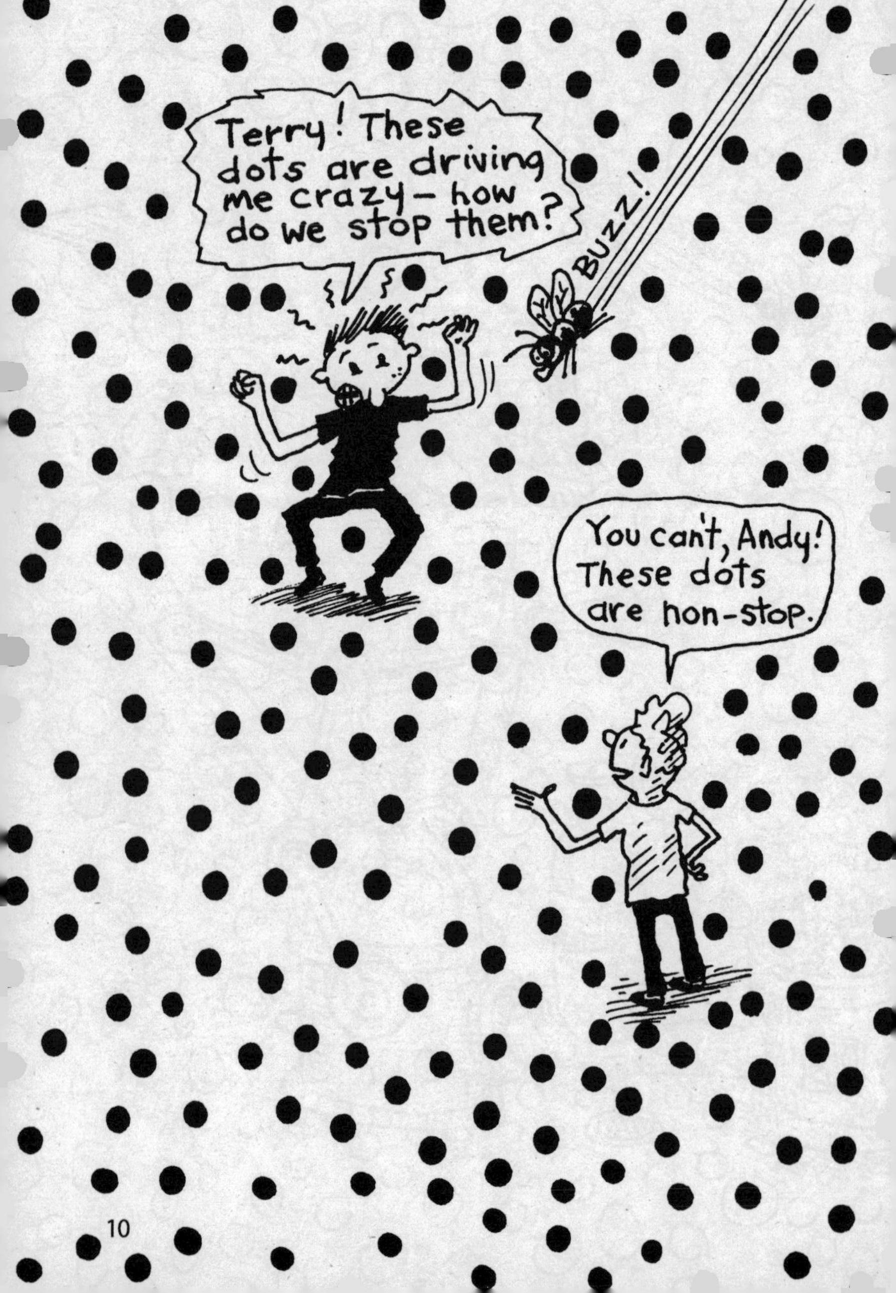

a 13-storey igloo,

11

the GRABINATOR (it can grab anything from anywhere at any time),

13

an extraterrestrial observation centre,

BUZZ!

15

a time-wasting level,

a toilet paper factory (because you can *never* have too much toilet paper),

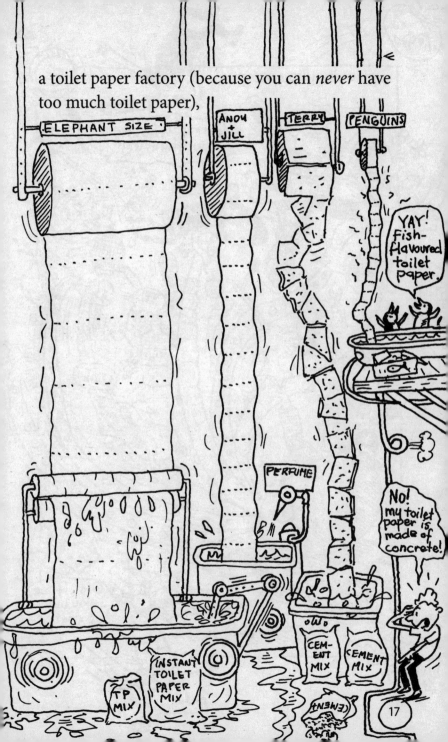

ELEPHANT SIZE

ANDY + JILL

TERRY

PENGUINS

YAY! Fish-flavoured toilet paper.

PERFUME

NO! my toilet paper is made of concrete!

TP MIX

INSTANT TOILET PAPER MIX

CEMENT MIX

CEMENT MIX

CEMENT

17

a soft grassy hill, perfect for rolling down,

a super long legs level,

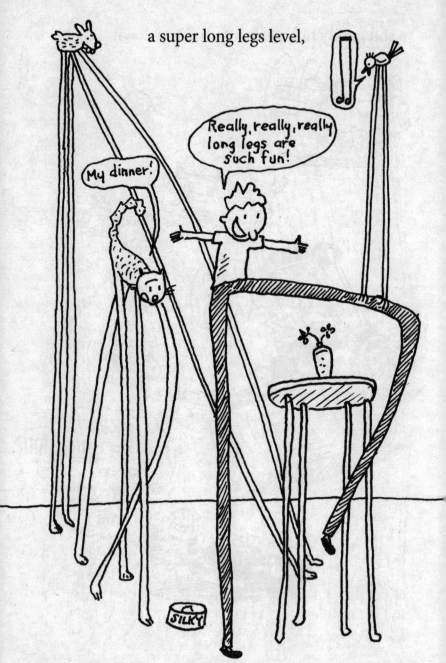

21

a TFB (that's short for
treehouse fire brigade),

Treehouse
fire
Brigade ↘

a people-eating plant called Petal,

and the best bookshop-in-a-treehouse-in-a-tree-in-a-forest-in-a-book in the whole world!

25

As well as being our home, the treehouse is where we make books together. I write the words and Terry draws the pictures.

As you can see, we've been doing
this for quite a while now.

Things don't always go to plan, of course …

but we always get our book done in the end.

CHAPTER 2

BUZZ! BUZZ! BUZZ!

If you're like most of our readers, you're probably wondering if we've ever been abducted by a giant flying eyeball from outer space. Well, it's funny you should be wondering that, because that's *exactly* what happened to us just the other day!

It all started when I was in the extraterrestrial observation centre. I was looking through the telescope trying to spot something that might give me an idea of what to write about in our next book when I came across the strangest-looking alien I'd ever seen!

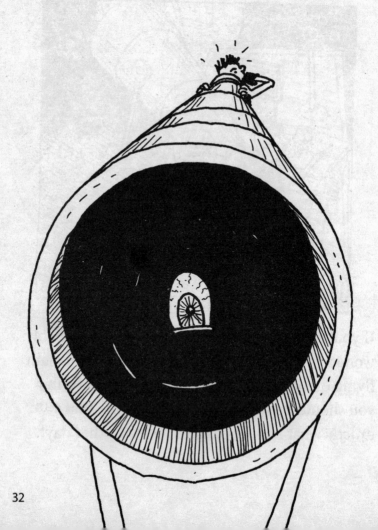

It had a hairy body with six legs, two wings and a weird trumpet thing sticking out the front of its face.

It was making a buzzing sound, kind of like a fly. Which wasn't surprising, really, because after a while I realised that's what it was—a fly, just an ordinary fly.

'Hey, get off my telescope!' I yelled. It did, but then it started buzzing around and around my head. At that moment I realised that this was no ordinary fly—this was a really *annoying* fly.

In the end I had no choice but to go and get …

THE SWATTER!

I swiped …

and swiped …

and swiped …

and swiped …

and swiped …

but it was no use. I couldn't *swat* it. That fly was not only really annoying, it was also really fast! I needed something bigger. So I went and got …

THE SUPER-SWATTER!

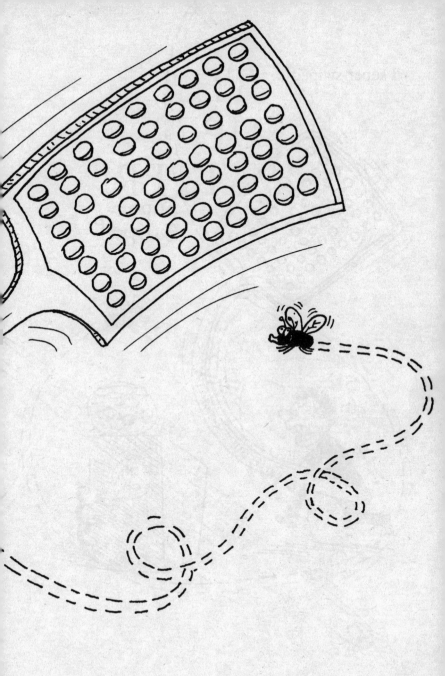

I super-swiped …

and super-swiped ...

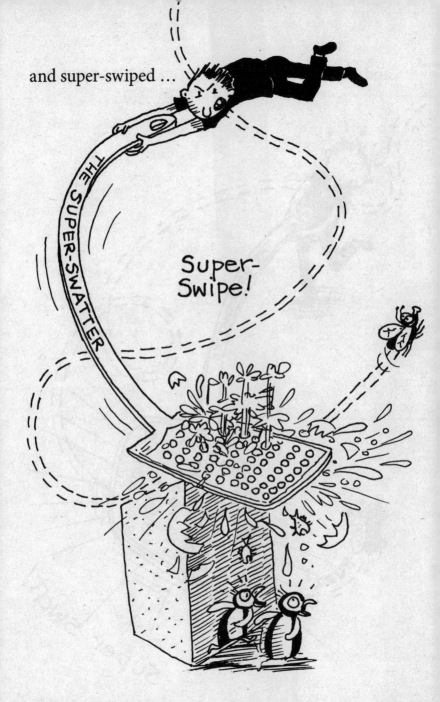

THE SUPER-SWATTER

Super-
Swipe!

and super-swiped again!

But no matter how much super-swiping I did,
I *still* couldn't swat that fly.

So I went and got …

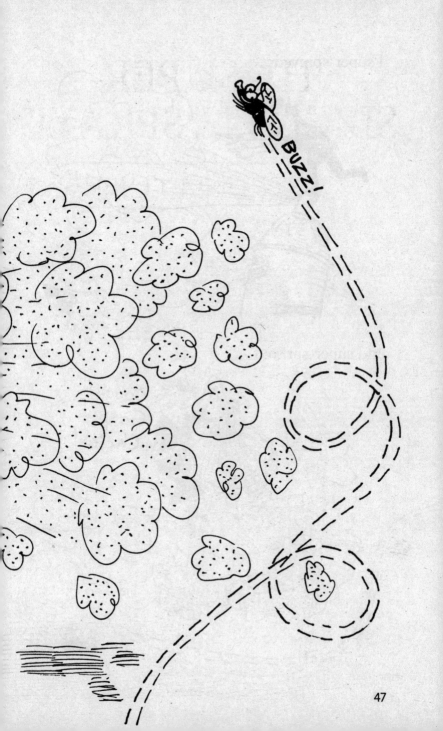

I super-sprayed ...

and super-sprayed ...

and super-sprayed!

I used up the whole can, but the fly was just as alive—and just as annoying—as ever! (I, on the other hand, was not feeling so great.)

The fly has not grown bigger, it's just a bit closer.

BUZZ

I had to get rid of that fly once and for all. It was time to unleash …

THE FLY
CANNON!

I had it lined up perfectly. I couldn't miss.

READY ...

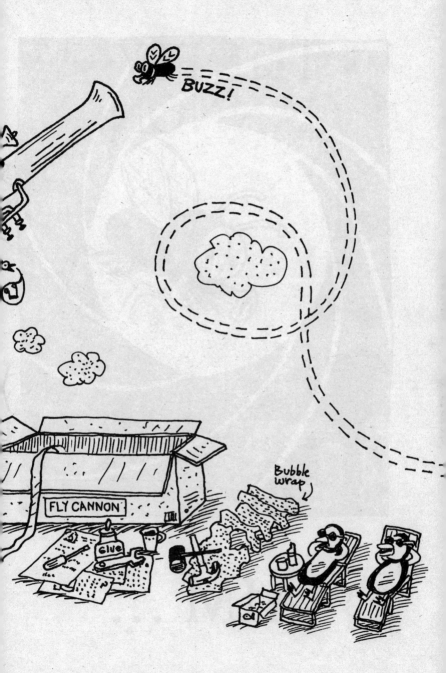

AIM ...

FIRE!

Like I said, I couldn't miss. But guess what? *I did!*
When the smoke cleared, there it was: that fly!
That REALLY ANNOYING fly.

BUZZ!

CHAPTER 3

FIRE!

'Hi, Andy,' said Terry. 'What's the matter?'

'That fly!' I said. 'That's what! I'm trying to get ideas for the next book but I can't because it keeps buzzing around my head and distracting me.'

'Have you tried swatting it?' said Terry.

'Yes,' I said. 'Of course I've tried swatting it!'

'Have you tried *super*-swatting it?'

'Yes!'

BUZZ!

'What about spraying it?'

'YES!' I said. 'I've tried *everything*, even blasting it with the fly cannon—but it didn't work. *Nothing* worked!'

'Maybe *I* can help,' said Terry. 'I could use my laser eyes!'

'Since when do you have laser eyes?' I said.

'Since this morning—when I invented them,' he said. 'Look, I'll show you.'

Terry took a deep breath, focused on the fly and shot laser beams at it—right out of his eyes!

The fly darted out of the way.

Terry took another deep breath and fired again …

and again …

and again ...

and again.

Terry's laser beams were hitting everything—
except for the fly, that is—and everything they
hit burst into flames.

'Terry!' I yelled. 'Stop! You're setting the
treehouse on fire!'

'Oops,' said Terry.

I grabbed an emergency bucket,
filled it with water and threw it
on one of the fires.

'Don't just stand there!' I said to Terry. 'Get a
bucket and help me!'

Terry grabbed the other emergency bucket and filled it with water.

'Oh no!' he said. 'It's leaking. There's a hole in my bucket!'

BUZZ!

'Then fix it!' I said.

'Hey, that reminds me of a song!' said Terry.

There's a hole in my bucket,
Dear Andy, dear Andy.
There's a hole in my bucket,
Dear Andy, a hole.

Before I knew it, I was singing, too. (It's a pretty catchy song.)

Suddenly, Jill came rushing in. 'FIRE! FIRE!'
she yelled. 'Your treehouse is on fire!'

'We know!' I said.

'Then why are you just standing around
singing? Why aren't you putting it out?'

BUZZ!

Because there's a hole in our bucket,
Dear Jill, dear Jill.
There's a hole in our bucket,
Dear Jill, there's a hole.

'Oh, for goodness sake!' said Jill. 'There's a *much* faster way to put out fires than by singing songs about buckets!'

She grabbed an emergency hammer and smashed the glass on our fire alarm.

FIRE

IN CASE
OF FIRE
BREAK
GLASS!

The siren wailed and, within moments, the treehouse fire brigade rushed in and got straight to work.

The Trunkinator was blasting water in all directions so fast it looked like he had three heads. (He didn't really have three heads, although I sort of wish he *did*: a three-headed elephant would be really cool!)

In no time at all, thanks to the brave firefighting crew, the fire was out and the tree was saved.

'Thank goodness for the treehouse fire brigade!' said Terry.

'And thank goodness for *me*,' said Jill. 'If I hadn't come along when I did you'd both still be singing that silly song while the treehouse burned down around you. Why was the treehouse on fire, anyway?'

'It was Terry's fault,' I said. 'He did it with his new laser eyes.'

'Laser eyes?' said Jill.

'Yeah,' said Terry. 'I have laser eyes. I can show you if you like.'

'NO, TERRY!' I said. 'They're too dangerous.'

'But what about the fly?' said Terry.
  'What fly?' said Jill.

'That really annoying one,' I said. 'It's driving me mad. I've tried swatting it, super-swatting it, super-spraying it and blasting it with the fly cannon, but it's no use. It won't die!'

'That *poor* fly,' said Jill.

'You mean that *annoying* fly,' I said.

'Buzz!' buzzed the fly from the branch just above my head.

'Nobody move,' I whispered. 'I have a plan.'

'You're not going to hurt it, are you?' said Jill.

'No chance of that,' I said. 'I *can't* hurt it. That fly is indestructible. I'm just going to give it a little holiday …

in my luxurious, super-modern, high-security
fly hotel!'

'Andy!' said Jill. 'That's not a *fly hotel*—it's a bug catcher. Let it out right now!'

'No way,' I said.

'But it's cruel,' said Jill. 'How would you like it if somebody trapped *you* in a bug catcher?'

'Well,' I said, 'I don't suppose I *would* like it—but as if *that's* going to happen!'

And then guess what? It *did* happen—well, something pretty similar to being trapped in a bug catcher, anyway. Suddenly, we found ourselves and our tree encased in a gigantic clear dome!

'Did you order a tree dome, Terry?' I said.

'No,' he said. 'Did you?'

'Not that I recall,' I said.

'Then where did it come from?' said Terry.

'I think it might have something to do with that UFE up there,' said Jill.

'Don't you mean UFO?' I said.

'No,' said Jill, pointing at a large oval object hovering above the tree. 'Look! It's definitely a UFE—an unidentified flying eyeball.'

'Wow!' said Terry. 'A giant flying eyeball! That's the coolest thing I've *ever* seen!'

CHAPTER 4

GOODBYE, EARTH

We stared up at the giant flying eyeball. It stared back down at us. Then the whole tree began to tremble and shake and rise up into the air.

'I didn't know our tree could fly,' said Terry.

'I don't think the tree is flying,' said Jill. 'I think the UFE is lifting it up! We're being abducted by a giant flying eyeball!'

'Yay!' said Terry. 'We're going on an intergalactic space adventure! I love intergalactic space adventures!'

'Me too!' I said. 'And just think of all the ideas we'll get for our next book!'

The higher we got, the faster we went, and, in what felt like no time at all, we had left Earth's atmosphere and entered outer space.

THE DAY WE WERE ABDUCTED BY A GIANT FLYING EYEBALL AND TAKEN ON A CRAZY RIDE THROUGH SPACE.

Thing 4

MERCURY

Black Hole

Grey Hole

VENUS

MOON

EARTH

MARS

JUPITER

Other Thing →

Albert 1

A bit falling off Jupiter

THE EDGE OF THE UNIVERSE

Albert 2

We were on the outer edge of the solar system
when the 3D video phone rang.

RING RING
RING RING
RING RING

I pushed the button to answer it. It was Mr Big
Nose, our publisher. His big nose filled the screen.

'What took you so long to answer the phone?' he yelled. 'Where were you?'

'We're in space,' I said. 'We just passed Uranus.'

'Are you trying to be funny?' said Mr Big Nose. 'I'm a busy man, you know. I don't have time for jokes!'

'No, it's not a joke,' I said. 'It's true! We really are in space.'

'What are you doing out there?' he shouted. 'You're supposed to be writing a book, remember?'

'I *do* remember,' I said, 'and I was trying to get ideas for it, but I couldn't because this really annoying fly was really annoying me, and then we got abducted by a giant flying eyeball!'

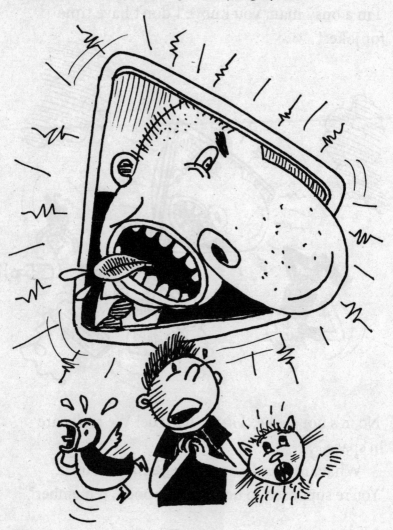

'A likely story!' said Mr Big Nose. 'But even if it *were* true, it's no excuse. Your book is due at five o'clock on Friday! And it had better be good. In fact, it had better be *better* than good—it had better be *out of this world*!'

'I think we can safely promise you that,' I said.

'What?' said Mr Big Nose. 'I can't see or h— you very well. You're br—king up.'

'You're breaking up, too,' I said.

'I'll br—k *you* up if — don't get your — to — on time!' yelled Mr Big Nose, and then the screen went blank.

'Goodbye, Mr Big Nose,' said Terry.

'Goodbye, solar system,' said Jill.

'What will we do now?' said Terry.

'Let's get started on the book,' I said. 'I've got a great idea for the beginning. Get this … I'm chasing a fly around, and then you come along and try to help but you set the treehouse on fire, and then Jill calls the treehouse fire brigade and then we—and our whole tree—get abducted by a giant flying eyeball!'

'Wow!' said Terry. 'I love it! Action-packed! What happens next? Where does the eyeball take us?'

'Well, I'm not too sure,' I said, 'because it hasn't happened yet. But I think we travel for a long time.'

'A *long* time?' said Terry. 'How long?'

'Not *too* long,' I said. 'And, um … it actually feels really short because we … we … we go to the time-wasting level and waste lots and lots of time, and soon all the time is wasted and we are there. Come on, let's go—there's no time to waste.'*

*Actually, as it turned out, there was … quite a lot, actually.

We began wasting time immediately. We started by tearing paper up into millions of tiny pieces and throwing them around to make snowstorms.

Then, when there was no more paper left, we decided to pop some bubble wrap. We must have popped at least ten million bubbles each!

After that, we made silly noises. We made every silly noise we could think of … and some that nobody had *ever* thought of!

And I don't know how much time we wasted doing online personality quizzes (but it was a LOT!).

After all that time-wasting we were feeling quite tired … and we'd only wasted one hour! So we decided to sit on the sofa and watch *Elephant on a Bicycle*.

We had a lot of trouble choosing an episode, though, because they're all so good—I mean, look at them! Which one would you have chosen?

Elephant on a Bicycle

SEASON ONE

Elephant on a Bicycle

ELEPHANT on a BICYCLE IN A CHINA SHOP

ELEPHANT on a BICYCLE AND THE ANGRY APE

ELEPHANT on a BICYCLE AND THE HUNGRY CATERPILLAR

ELEPHANT on a BICYCLE AND THE BIG WET WATERFALL

ELEPHANT on a BICYCLE AND THE GIANT RABBIT

ELEPHANT on a BICYCLE AND THE FERAL CHAINSAW

Elephant on a Bicycle

SEASON THREE

ELEPHANT on a BICYCLE JOINS THE CIRCUS

ELEPHANT on a BICYCLE AND THE ROBBERS

ELEPHANT on a BICYCLE AND THE CURIOUS KITTEN

ELEPHANT on a BICYCLE ON THE FARM

ELEPHANT on a BICYCLE AND THE CUP OF FIRE

ELEPHANT on a BICYCLE AND THE MYSTERY OF THE MISSING WHEEL

Elephant on a Bicycle

Elephant on a Bicycle

ELEPHANT on a BICYCLE
AT THE SEASIDE

ELEPHANT on a BICYCLE
TO THE RESCUE

ELEPHANT on a BICYCLE
AND THE BIG HOLE

ELEPHANT on a BICYCLE
AND THE BEANSTALK

ELEPHANT on a BICYCLE
AND HUMPTY DUMPTY'S
BIG FALL

ELEPHANT on a BICYCLE
AND THE GARBAGE TRUCK

Elephant on a Bicycle

Elephant on a Bicycle

SEASON SEVEN

ELEPHANT on a BICYCLE AND THE VERY BUMPY ROAD

ELEPHANT on a BICYCLE AND THE PIRATES

ELEPHANT on a BICYCLE IN UPSIDE-DOWN LAND

ELEPHANT on a BICYCLE AND THE BIRTHDAY CAKE

ELEPHANT on a BICYCLE MEETS BARKY THE BARKING DOG

ELEPHANT on a BICYCLE VS ZOMBIES

Elephant on a Bicycle

ELEPHANT on a BICYCLE IN OUTER SPACE

ELEPHANT on a BICYCLE ON ICE

ELEPHANT on a BICYCLE MEETS THE 3 SHARKS

ELEPHANT on a BICYCLE AND THE GIANT EAGLES

ELEPHANT on a BICYCLE AND THE DEEP BLUE SEA

ELEPHANT on a BICYCLE MEETS GODZILLA

Obviously, it was impossible to choose just one, so we ended up watching the entire series in order from the first episode to the very last!

'Gee, we sure have wasted a *lot* of time,' said Terry
when it was finished.

'Yes,' said Jill. 'I wonder if we're there yet.'

'Where?' I said.

'Wherever it is we're going,' said Jill.

'There's a planet out there that looks just like a giant eyeball,' said Terry. 'Maybe *that's* where we're going.'

As it turned out, that's *exactly* where we were going.

'Hold tight, everyone,' said Jill. 'We're going in.'

CHAPTER 5

EYEBALLIA

We must have all blacked out for a while because the next thing we knew we were all lying on the ground beside our tree. We got up and looked around. That's when we realised we were being watched by …

MILLIONS OF EYEBALLS!!

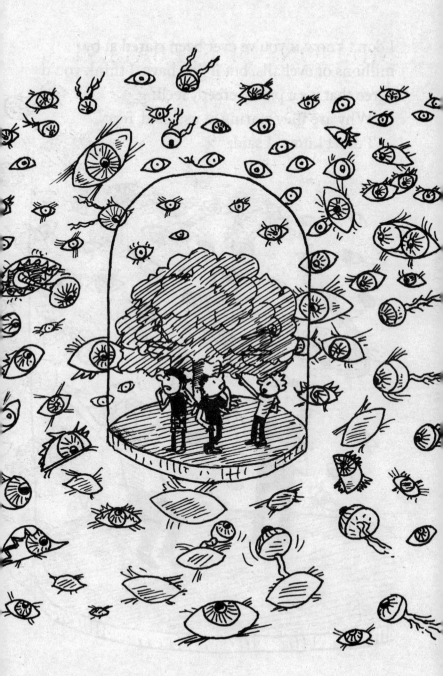

I don't know if you've ever been stared at by millions of eyeballs, but if you have, I think you'd agree that it's a pretty creepy feeling.

'Why are they staring at us?' said Terry.

'I don't know,' I said.

'It's not just us they're staring at,' called Jill, who had climbed to the observation deck at the top of the tree. 'Come up here and see.'

We climbed up. There were domes all around us— each one containing a different species of alien and surrounded by crowds of staring eyeballs.

'Oh no,' I said. 'This is terrible! We're exhibits in an intergalactic zoo!'

'I hate zoos!' said Terry. 'Some intergalactic space adventure this is turning out to be!'

'I know it's not great,' said Jill, 'but it could be worse. At least we're not contestants in one of those intergalactic death battles.'

'What intergalactic death battles?' I said.

'You know,' said Jill, 'those ones where some sort of evil aliens collect specimens from other planets and then make them fight each other ... to the death.'

'I thought that just happened in comic books,' said Terry.

'No, I'm pretty sure it's a real thing,' said Jill.

'Well, let's hope it's not,' I said. 'Because some of those aliens look really mean. I think that one over there is a razor-toothed, blood-sucking Venusian worm man. I wouldn't even want to be in a dance contest with him, let alone a battle to the death!'

above: *An artist's impression of Andy and a razor-toothed, blood-sucking Venusian worm man having a dance contest.*

'Look,' said Terry. 'There's an absolutely enormous eyeball up there. That's the biggest one I've seen so far!'

'Attention all specimens!' said the giant eyeball.
'Wow!' said Terry. 'A talking eyeball—cool!'

'Congratulations!' the eyeball continued. 'You have been chosen to represent your planet in Eyeballia's intergalactic death battle. The winner will receive an attractive trophy, and every participant will receive a commemorative participation medal. The battle will begin in five minutes. Good luck—and may the best species win!'

CHAPTER 6

INTERGALACTIC DEATH BATTLE

'Did you hear that?' said Terry.

'Yes,' I said. 'We're all going to die in an intergalactic death battle!'

'No,' said Terry, 'not *that* bit. The bit about how we could win a trophy—or a medal!'

'Unless we lose, that is,' I said.

'No, Andy,' said Terry. 'You don't understand. Even if we lose, we still get a medal that says: *If you had fun, you won!*'

'No,' I said. '*You* don't understand. A death battle is a battle to the *death*. Only the winner survives: the losers—which is everybody else—will all *die*.'

'Then we'd better make sure we win,' said Terry.

'But that would mean we have to kill all the other contestants,' said Jill. 'That's *awful*!'

She has very long legs.

'It's less awful than being killed,' said Terry. 'And it's not like we have a choice.'

'But how could we win even if we wanted to?' said Jill. 'The other aliens look *much* more dangerous than us. We don't stand a chance!'

'You're forgetting one very important thing,' said Terry. 'Well, two, actually. I have laser eyes.'

'But you can't even kill a *fly* with your laser eyes!' I said. 'How do you expect them to help us win an intergalactic death battle?'

As we were speaking, thousands of flying eyeballs were filling the air around us.

'Attention all aliens,' boomed the giant flying eyeball. 'In a moment your enclosures will be removed and the battle will begin. It will continue until only one species remains. Are there any questions?'

'Yes,' said a little green blob. 'Please may I be excused from the battle? I need to go home.'

'No,' said the eyeball. 'All contestants must fight. It's the rules.'

Then, without warning, the eyeball let out a loud, high-pitched noise and our enclosure shattered. In fact, all the enclosures did.

We got such a fright, we fell out of the tree onto the soft spongy surface of Eyeballia with all the other aliens.

It was terrifying being so close to so many dangerous aliens, but there was hardly any time to feel scared, because then the eyeball said:

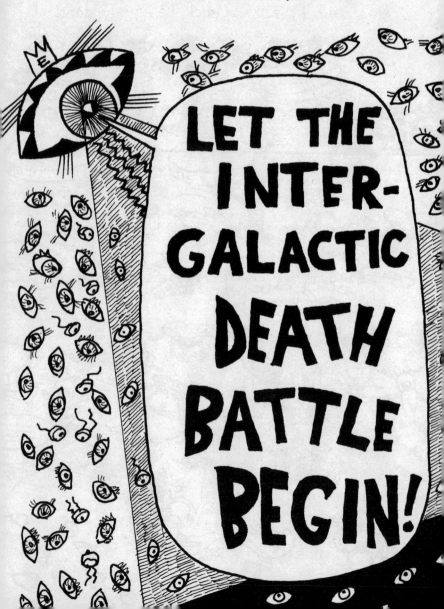

We all jumped up.

'Oh no!' said Jill. 'What are we going to do?'

'Fight?' said Terry.

'No,' I said. 'Let's hide! Quick! Behind the door!'

'The Door of Doom?' said Terry. 'Are you crazy?'

'No!' I said. 'The *front* door!'

We all rushed inside—and not a moment too soon, because then …

the battle began!

133

'I don't think I like intergalactic death battles very much,' I said, as the battle raged around our tree.

'Me neither,' said Jill. 'They're quite violent.'

'And they're too loud,' said Terry. 'I wish we could go home.'

'Unfortunately, that's not an option,' I said. 'But let's look on the bright side. Perhaps, with a bit of luck, they'll all destroy each other without us having to do anything or hurt anyone, and then we can collect the trophy and get out of here.'

'Not much hope of that,' said Jill, pointing at a hideous bull-like alien that was charging towards the tree. 'I think that one's realised we're in here.'

'This would be a perfect time to use your laser eyes, Terry!' I yelled. 'Blast it!'

'I can't!' he said. 'I'm too scared. My eyes won't even open!'

At that moment, Mary Lollipoppins pushed past us, her hands full of enormous lollipops.

'Never fear!' she cried. 'LOLLIPOPPINS is here!'

The alien roared at Mary, but she just laughed and said, 'My, what a big gob you have, Grandma—just the right size for these super-sticky, super-giant, all-day gob-stoppers!' and as quick as a lollipop-shop robot, she shoved all four lollipops into the alien's open mouth. It was too surprised to continue its attack and too busy sucking on the gob-stoppers to do us any harm at all.

'Good work, Mary!' shouted Jill. 'But watch out behind you!'

A razor-toothed, blood-sucking Venusian worm man was standing right behind Mary, about to bite her head off, when a scoop of hot ice-cream smashed into its face.

SPLAT!

'Never fear! SCOOPERHANDS is also here!' yelled Edward Scooperhands from above as he launched scoopful after scoopful of sizzling hot ice-cream at the worm man.

The razor-toothed, blood-sucking Venusian worm man reared back and howled in pain. Or was it pleasure? It was hard to tell. It could have been either—or both. Hot ice-cream is hot, sure, but it's also delicious.

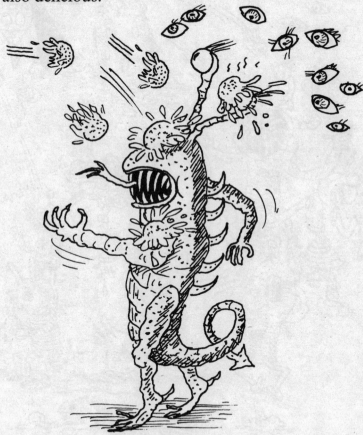

So delicious, in fact, that all the other aliens stopped fighting the death battle …

and started having a hot ice-cream
party instead!

CHAPTER 7

INTERGALACTIC HOT ICE-CREAM PARTY

The aliens weren't the only ones enjoying the hot ice-cream party—Jill and Terry joined in as well. They were jumping around, trying to catch fresh scoops of hot ice-cream in their hands and mouths just as fast as Edward could throw them.

'Attention all aliens!' announced the giant eyeball. 'May I remind you, this is an *intergalactic death battle*, not an intergalactic hot ice-cream party. Resume fighting immediately!'

But the aliens took absolutely no notice—except for one, which looked up at the eyeball and spat hot ice-cream right at it.

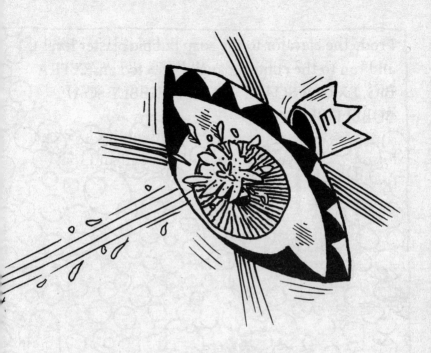

It was a direct hit—the hot ice-cream hit the eyeball right in the … well … right in the eyeball!

It went all bloodshot and watery and was obviously in a lot of pain.

That's when I had an idea.

It was possibly one of the greatest ideas I've ever had. Possibly one of the greatest ideas *anybody* has *ever* had in the history of people having great ideas!

I rode the elevator to the soap bubble blaster level and ran to the control panel. I selected an EXTRA BIG, EXTRA SOAPY, EXTRA BUBBLY SOAP BUBBLE BLIZZARD.

The machine rumbled and grumbled ...

shuddered and shook ...

OINK!

and blasted out a blinding blizzard of bubbles—thousands and millions and billions of bubbles.

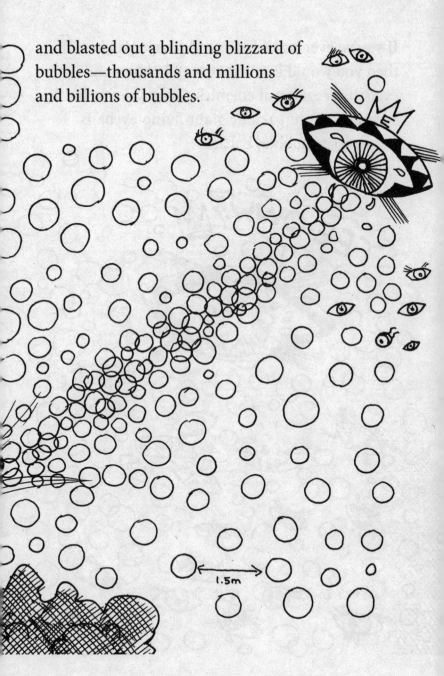

1.5m

If you've ever had a bath (and I hope you have!), then you would know that soap bubbles and eyeballs are natural enemies. So now a new battle started: an intergalactic giant-flying-eyeballs versus soap-bubbles battle!

And it was a battle the soap bubbles were clearly winning. The eyeballs—blinded and driven mad by the stinging—were just flying around, crashing into each other and bursting like huge bags of watery jelly (which is not surprising, really, because that's exactly what giant eyeballs are).

Meanwhile, the aliens took advantage of the mayhem and made a run for it.

'Hey, Andy!' said Terry when I returned to the battlefield. 'You'll never guess what just happened!'

'Let me try,' I said. 'A soap bubble blizzard stung all the eyeballs and the aliens made a run for it?'

'YES!' said Terry. 'How did you know?'

'Because, while you and Jill were busy having a hot ice-cream party, it was *me* who started the blizzard!'

'Great idea, Andy!' said Jill.

'I know!' I said.

'I've got a great idea, too,' said Terry. 'Let's get out of here!'

'I'd like nothing better than to leave this eyeball-infested planet,' I said. 'But how? Our tree is an amazing tree, but it's not a rocket.'

'If only I had my yo-yo,' said Terry.

'What possible use would a yo-yo be to us now?' I said.

'Well, it could help to pass the time for one thing,' Terry said. 'But, more importantly, the yo-yo I ordered on yoBay last week came with four free rocket boosters. We could have attached them to the tree and blasted off.'

BEEP!
BEEP!

'Hey,' said Terry. 'That sounds like Bill the postman's scooter horn.'

'It does,' I said. 'But what would Bill be doing out here on Eyeballia?'

'Delivering the mail, of course!' called a voice that sounded just like Bill's … and there was a good reason for that, and that's because it *was* Bill's.

'I have a parcel for Terry, which I tried to deliver, but just as I arrived your tree took off. So I followed you.'

'You followed us into space and all the way to Eyeballia?' said Jill.

'Well, I had no choice,' said Bill. 'When I became a postman I swore an oath to deliver the mail no matter *where* and no matter *what*.'

Bill put a hand on his heart and began reciting his oath:

No matter how near,
No matter how far,

Whether the house next door,
Or the farthest star,

No matter how high,
No matter how low,

Where the mail is addressed
That's where I go.

Neither heat of day,
Nor gloom of night,

Neither birds that swoop,
Nor dogs that bite,

Neither cats that scratch,
Nor scary ghost,

paper bag

Shall EVER prevent me
From delivering the post.

Neither snow nor rain,
Nor cannon blast,

Boom!

Neither killer bees,
Nor plaster cast,

BOING!

Neither yetis nor dragons,
Nor storm of hail,

Grrr!

Shall EVER prevent me
From delivering the mail.

Bill took his hand off his heart and wiped a tear from his eye. 'As you can see,' he said, 'I take my job very seriously.'

He reached into his mail bag and pulled out a small parcel. 'Here's the yo-yo you ordered, Terry.'

'And here are your three bonus rocket boosters.
There were four but I borrowed one to get here.
I hope you don't mind.'

'I don't mind at all,' said Terry. 'Thank you, Bill,
you're the greatest postman in the whole world!'

'You mean the whole *universe*,' said Jill.

'I don't know about that,' chuckled Bill. 'Just
doing my job.'

It didn't take long to strap the rocket boosters to the trunk of the tree. (We didn't have straps so we used heavy duty toilet paper instead. Don't worry, it was fireproof as well.)

'Prepare for lift-off,' I said.

There was a massive *whoosh* as we shot up through Eyeballia's atmosphere and out into space.

'Goodbye, Eyeballia,' I yelled above the roar of the rocket boosters.

'And good riddance!' yelled Jill.

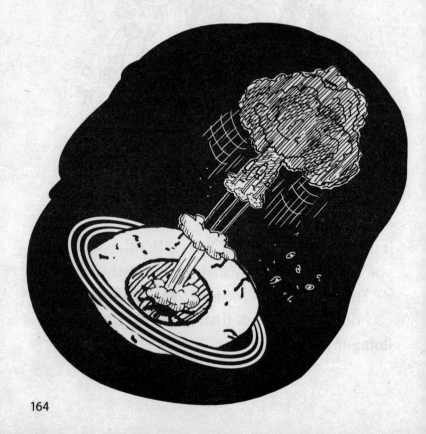

CHAPTER 8

STOWAWAY!

'Wait!' said Terry. 'Turn the tree around! We have to go back!'

'Why?' I said.

'We didn't get our participation medals!'

'Yes, we did,' said Jill. 'I grabbed them as we left—one for each of us, including Edward Scooperhands and Mary Lollipoppins.'

'Oh well,' said Bill. 'This has been quite an adventure but I'd better be getting along. This mail won't deliver itself, you know.'

'Why don't you hitch a ride back to Earth with us?' I said.

'It's very kind of you,' said Bill, 'but I've got a few letters addressed to the Andromeda Galaxy that I need to deliver before I head home.'

'All right,' I said. 'But be careful out there—and watch out for giant flying eyeballs!'

'I will,' shouted Bill over the roar of his rocket-boosted scooter as he soared off into space.

'Well, I'm glad that's over,' said Terry. 'I think I've had enough space adventure for one book.'

'Me too,' I said. 'In fact, I'd be happy if I never saw another alien for as long as I live.'

'Well, don't look under the table then,' said Jill.

'Why not?' I said.

'Because there's a little green blob hiding under there.'

'Code green!' I yelled. 'Repeat: code green!'
     'What's code green again?' said Terry.

'Alien stowaway!' I yelled as the blob darted out
from under the table. 'Blast it, Terry—give it
both eyes!'

Terry focused, took aim and fired two deadly laser beams at the blob.

There was no way he could miss from this close … and he didn't. It was a direct hit!

What we hadn't counted on, though, was that the blob had the ability to change shape ... and it did!

No sooner had Terry fired than the blob transformed itself into a mirror and bounced the lasers right back at us!

We all ducked, and just in time too—the laser beams were so close you could feel the heat coming off them as they shot over us!

Terry stood up and faced the blob. 'So you want to fight, do you?' he said.

'No,' pleaded the blob, which had gone back to being a blob again. 'I *don't* want to fight!'

'Well, you should have thought about that before you attacked us,' said Terry.

'I didn't attack you!' said the blob. 'You started it. I was just protecting myself.'

'It's a fair point,' said Jill. 'Maybe we should give the blob the benefit of the doubt. We can't be *sure* that it was trying to hurt us.'

'And we can't be sure it wasn't,' I said. 'I say we catapult this slimy little shape-shifter into space right now!'

'Not so fast, Andy,' said Jill.

She turned to the blob. 'What are you doing here?' she said. 'Why did you stow away on our tree?'

'I had to!' said the blob. 'I have to get back home to Blobdromeda. Everybody there is in terrible danger and it's all my fault! I have to save them!'

'Why?' said Terry. 'What's wrong?'

'Well,' said the little blob, 'it's a long story …'

'Oh good,' said Terry. 'I love long stories!'

We all sat down and the blob began.

Once upon a time, on a small muddy planet called Blobdromeda, there lived a bunch of mud-loving blobs that were as happy as a bunch of mud-loving blobs could be. All day long they swam in mud ...

wrestled in mud ...

sang songs about mud ...

MUD, GLORIOUS MUD,
WET, OOZY AND SLIMY.
BOGS, QUICKSAND AND SWAMPS,
OH, HOW WE LOVE TO BE GRIMY.

and made the muddiest and most delicious mud pies you could ever imagine!

There was only one thing the blobs had to worry about: the great mud-sucking bog toad.

The great mud-sucking bog toad lived in a bog and—as you can guess from its name—it also loved mud. It would have sucked up all the mud that the blobs lived in, if it weren't for the fact that the only thing it loved more than sucking up mud was eating freshly made mud pies. Which is how an ancient tradition began ...

On the first mud moon of each mud month, the blobs would make an extra-massive, extra-muddy mud pie for the bog toad. In return for the pie, the bog toad did not suck up all their mud.

On the night of the most recent mud moon, however, a terrible thing happened. All the blobs had left the pie out for the bog toad, as usual, and then went to sleep in the mud, except for one blob that remained on duty to guard the pie.

It was the blob's first time on pie-guarding duty and, as the hours dragged on, it became very hungry. The extra-massive, extra-muddy mud pie looked so good shining in the moonlight that the blob couldn't resist eating just a tiny bit.

The mud pie tasted every bit as good as it looked!
Crunchy on the outside, soft and gooey on
the inside. In fact, it tasted so good, the blob
decided to have just a tiny bit more …

and then another tiny bit more …

and then another and another tiny bit more ...

and then another and another and another tiny
bit more ... until there was nothing left of the
mud pie but a few muddy crumbs.

The blob was ashamed of what it had done, but there was no time to confess and ask the rest of the blobs to help make another mud pie because, at that moment, the great mud-sucking bog toad appeared!

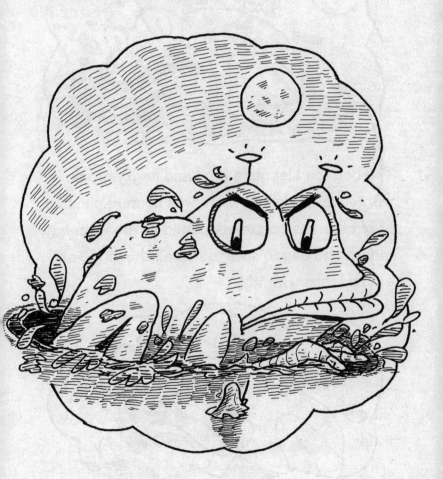

The bog toad looked around for the mud pie but, of course, it couldn't see it because it was in the blob's stomach.

The bog toad let out a loud and angry croak. It wanted mud pie, but there was no mud pie! In a fit of rage, the bog toad opened its great greedy mouth and began sucking up all the mud—and all the blobs with it!

The bog toad kept sucking until it had sucked
up all the mud and all the blobs.

'*All* the blobs?' said Jill. 'Even the blob that ate
the pie?'

'Well, no,' said the blob. 'All the blobs *except*
the blob that ate the pie.'

'Wait a minute,' said Terry, 'if there was only one blob left and *you're* telling the story, then does that mean *you* are the blob that ate the mud pie?'

'Yes,' said the blob, 'I'm sorry to say that I am.'

'I *knew* it!' said Terry.

'But how did you end up on Eyeballia?' I said.

'Well,' said the blob, 'just after the bog toad had sucked up all the blobs—before I could do anything to save them—I was abducted by a giant flying eyeball and taken to Eyeballia to fight in the intergalactic death battle.'

187

'That's exactly like what happened to us!' said Terry. 'Well, not the bit about the bog toad and the mud and the pie, but *we* were abducted by a giant flying eyeball, too.'

'Those eyeballs sure have a nerve,' said Jill. 'How dare they fly around the universe abducting whoever they like for their horrible intergalactic death battles! I'm *so* glad we got away from them.'

'Don't speak too soon,' I said. 'Look! They're coming after us!'

189

'Yikes!' said Terry. 'Can't this tree go any faster?'
   'I don't think the speed of the tree is the real
problem here,' said Jill. 'Or the fact that we're
being chased by a bunch of angry eyeballs.
The real problem is that we're headed straight
towards that sun!'

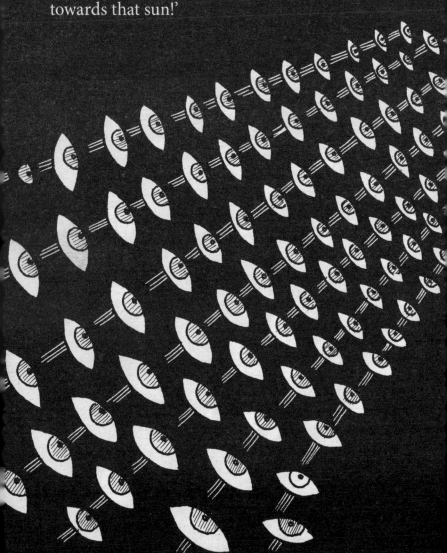

'Oh no!' said Terry. 'We're doomed!'

'Maybe,' I said. 'But then again, maybe not.'

'How do you figure that?' said Jill.

'Well,' I said, 'I've just done a few quick calculations and it would appear that, based on our current speed and trajectory, our tree is going to narrowly miss that sun, whereas the eyeballs are travelling much faster and will not be able to change course in time. They'll burn up long before they're able to catch us.'

'Are you sure about that?' said Jill.

'I am,' I said. 'Look out there if you don't believe me.'

Just as I had predicted, the eyeballs began bursting into flames.

CHAPTER 9

FLAMING EYEBALLS

'FLAMING EYEBALLS!' yelled Terry. 'You were right, Andy—they're burning up!'

'Those poor eyeballs,' said Jill.

'Are you kidding?' I said. 'Those *poor eyeballs* were happy to see us fight each other to the death just for their amusement.'

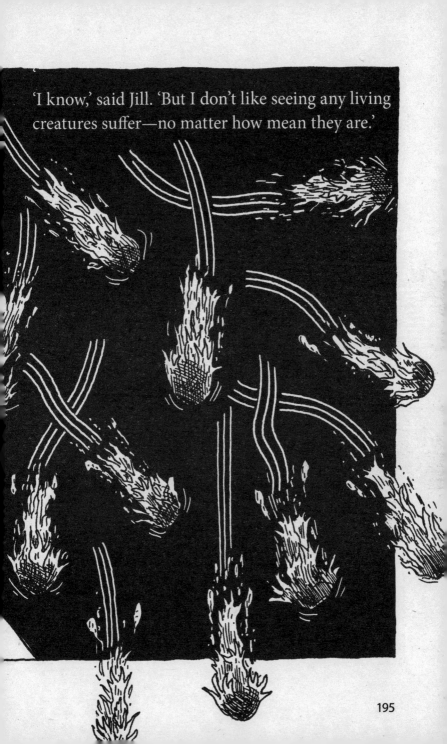

'I know,' said Jill. 'But I don't like seeing any living creatures suffer—no matter how mean they are.'

'That worked out pretty well,' said Terry after the last of the eyeballs had flamed out of view. 'We defeated the giant flying eyeballs, and have put an end to their intergalactic death battles forever. The aliens of the universe can now live in peace, free from the fear of being abducted by eyeballs, and it's all thanks to us!'

'There's just one small problem,' said Jill, wiping sweat from her brow. 'Well, one *big* problem, really. We seem to be getting awfully close to the sun ourselves. Are you sure your calculations are correct, Andy?'

'Of course I am,' I said. 'But you can check them if you want.'

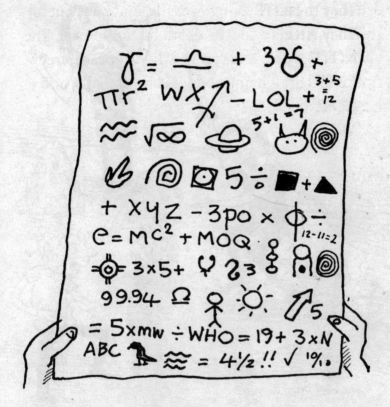

Terry took the page from my hand and examined it. 'These aren't calculations,' he said. 'It's just scribble!'

'No, it's not,' I said. 'It just seems like that to you because you don't understand astrology. My calculations are far beyond your comprehension.'

'No, they're not,' said Terry.

'Yes, they are,' I said.

'They're NOT!'

'They ARE!'

'NOT!'

'ARE!'

'NOT!'

'ARE!'

As you can see, I was easily winning the argument—well, that was until we got so close to the sun that the page of calculations started smoking and then caught fire in Terry's hand. 'Ouch!' he said as he dropped it and stamped out the flames.

'It's getting *really* hot!' said Jill. 'I feel like I'm melting—in fact, I think I *am* melting!'

'Me too,' said Terry. 'My legs have gone all soft.'

I was starting to melt, too. I mean, it was hot! And when I say 'it was hot', I mean it was REALLY hot. And when I say 'it was REALLY hot', I mean it was REALLY REALLY hot! But just when we thought we couldn't take it any more, we didn't have to … because, suddenly, the treehouse was covered in shade—cool, dark shade.

'I didn't know the treehouse had an emergency sun umbrella,' said Jill.

'Neither did I,' said Terry. 'Did you put it in, Andy?'

'No,' I said.

'Then where's all that shade coming from?' said Jill.

'It's the blob!' said Terry. 'It's turned itself into a giant sun umbrella and it's shading the entire tree!'

'Thank you, Blob!' I shouted.

THE DAY THE BLOB TURNED
ITSELF INTO A GIANT SUN
UMBRELLA AND SAVED US
ALL FROM BURNING UP.

202

As it turned out, my calculations were right: we didn't actually fly into the sun—but we did go very close. If it hadn't been for the blob, we wouldn't have survived.

The poor blob, however, was in a bad way. It fell back down into the treehouse, exhausted. It was completely dried up and cracked, like a lump of plasticine that's been left out of its container for too long.

'We need to get this blob rehydrated at once,' said Dr Moose.

(You might remember Dr Moose from our last book, *The 117-Storey Treehouse*. He writes books, too, but he's also a doctor. He liked our treehouse so much that he decided to stay on as our chief medical officer.)

Dr Moose put the blob in a bed and attached it to a saline drip.

We all crowded around.

'Do you think it will be all right, Doctor?' said Jill.

Well, I'm not sure if blobs eat fish... but I'll ask.

'It's hard to say,' said Dr Moose. 'Its vital signs are not good. Flexibility is poor, breathing is shallow and it's very close to completely cracking up. It also has the worst case of sunburn I've ever seen.'

The little blob opened its eyes and looked up at us.

'Did we make it past the sun?' it said weakly.

'Yes,' said Jill. 'Thanks to you! You're a hero. You saved us all from burning up.'

'Thank goodness,' said the blob in a rasping voice. 'I'm glad everybody's okay, but I'm afraid it's all over for me. I'm all dried up. Now I'll never get back to Blobdromeda to put things right and save my friends and family from the belly of the mud-sucking bog toad.'

'Maybe we could save them for you,' said Terry.

'Would you really do that?' said the blob.

'Of course,' I said. 'It's the least we could do after what you've done for us. I just wish we could save you, too.'

'Never mind about me,' whispered the blob. 'I'm just one blob—and a bad one at that—but it gives me great comfort to know that everybody on Blobdromeda will soon be free to sing and wallow in the mud again and, Blob willing, will do so forever more.'

The blob closed its eyes.

'Wait,' I said. 'Where exactly *is* Blobdromeda?'

The blob took a big breath and said, 'Blobdromeda is in the eighth dimension … of the fourth quadrant … near the twenty-fifth sector … of the ninety-third nebula … of the eighth arm of the twenty-second supercluster—you can't miss it.'

The blob fell back onto the pillow and then, exhausted, cracked into pieces and crumbled into dust.

'I'm afraid it's all over for this little blob,' said Dr Moose. He gently gathered the blob's remains, placed them in a shoebox and handed it to Terry.

We carried the shoebox to the beautiful sunny meadow, where Edward Scooperhands helped us to scoop out a shallow grave.

We lowered the shoebox into it, and I recited a short poem in the blob's honour.

'I didn't know the blob for long,' said Jill, wiping away tears, 'but I'll really miss it. Sure, it shouldn't have eaten that mud pie, but it had a good heart. I hope we can help all its friends and family on Blobdromeda.'

'Of course we will,' I said. 'And the sooner we get there, the sooner we can set those blobs free.'

'Let's go!' said Terry. 'To Blobdromeda and beyond!'

'Actually, not beyond,' I corrected him. 'We just want to get to Blobdromeda.'

'Got it!' said Terry. 'To Blobdromeda—AND NO FURTHER!'

CHAPTER 10

BLOBDROMEDA

We travelled through the eighth dimension of the fourth quadrant …

past the twenty-fifth sector of the ninety-third
nebula of the eighth arm of the twenty-second
supercluster …

and there was Blobdromeda, right where the little blob said it would be!

'We made it!' said Terry.

The surface of Blobdromeda looked pretty rocky, and it appeared we were in for a rough landing, so we decided to take shelter in the room full of pillows.

We had only just arrived in the room full of
pillows when Terry said what he always says when
we go there: 'Hey, I've got a good idea—let's have a
pillow fight!'

'No way,' I said. 'This may be the place but it's
hardly the time. We're on a mission—all those blobs
trapped in the bog toad are depending on us!'

'You're right, Andy,' said Terry. 'This is no time for games.' And then he whomped me with a pillow.

So I whomped him back.

Jill whomped us both—

and the great intergalactic pillow fight was on!

The pillow fight was still raging as we landed on Blobdromeda's boulder-strewn surface.

'Everyone okay?' I said.

'I'm fine,' said Terry, emerging from underneath a pile of pillows.

'Me too,' said Jill. 'But that was some jolt!'

'Can anybody see the bog toad?' said Terry.

'No,' said Jill, 'but I can smell it. In fact, we're right on top of it.'

'Yikes!' said Terry. 'We're on top of a bog toad!'

'Yes,' said Jill. 'And, unless I'm very much mistaken, those rocks and boulders aren't rocks and boulders—they're bog toad warts.'

'Bog toad warts?' I said. 'How disgusting!'

'Look on the bright side,' said Jill. 'At least we're on the outside of this bog toad and not on the inside like those poor blobs.'

We climbed down off the bog toad, which was surprisingly easy, because although the bog toad warts were disgusting, they also made excellent foot- and handholds.

'That was fun,' said Terry when we reached the ground. 'We should build a wart-climbing wall in our treehouse.'

'Yeah,' I said. 'But where would we get the warts from?'

'We can make them in our secret underground laboratory,' said Terry.

'Of course,' I said.

We walked around to the front of the bog toad and stared at it.

It stared back at us.

We stared back at the bog toad.

'Anyone know how to get blobs out of a bog toad?' I said.

'We need to make it open its mouth,' said Jill. 'Perhaps we could try making it laugh. Does anybody know any good bog toad jokes?'

'I know one,' said Terry, turning to the bog toad. 'Hey, you, bog toad, do you want to hear a joke?'

The bog toad just stared at him.

'All right, then,' said Terry, 'I'll take that as a *yes*.'

The bog toad blinked.

Terry began: 'A person was at the cinema when they noticed what looked like a bog toad sitting next to them. "Excuse me," said the person, "are you a bog toad?"

'"Yes, I am," said the bog toad.

'"What are you doing at the cinema?" said the person.

'"Well," said the bog toad, "I liked the book."'

We all laughed. Well, all of us except for the bog toad. It just stared at Terry.

Terry turned to us. 'I don't understand why it's not laughing,' he said. 'That's a really funny joke.'

'Maybe it doesn't know what a movie is,' said Jill.

'Maybe it doesn't know what a book is,' I said.

'Or maybe bog toads just don't have a sense of humour,' said Terry.

'Are bog toads ticklish?' I said.

'I'm not sure,' said Jill. 'But there's a good way to find out. Let's tickle it. Ready, set, go!'

We team-tickled the bog toad with everything
we had—our fingers, feathers, feather dusters, an
electric toothbrush and even a vacuum cleaner …

but nothing worked. The bog toad didn't even
smile, let alone open its mouth to laugh.

'Hmmm,' I said. 'I think we can safely conclude that this bog toad does not have a sense of humour and is not ticklish. Unless we can think of some other way to make it open its mouth, the blobs are doomed!'

Just then I heard a buzzing sound. A really *annoying* buzzing sound.

The fly was back! And it was even louder and more annoying than it was before!

BUZZ!
BUZZ!
BUZZ!

'Who let that fly out?' I said.

'I did,' said Jill. 'I thought it could help.'

'Help?' I said. 'It's not going to help—it's just going to fly around and annoy us all!'

'Exactly!' said Jill. 'I'm hoping it's going to annoy the bog toad as well.'

The fly buzzed dangerously close to the bog toad's head. It was hard to tell if the bog toad was getting annoyed or not, but it was definitely watching the fly with great interest.

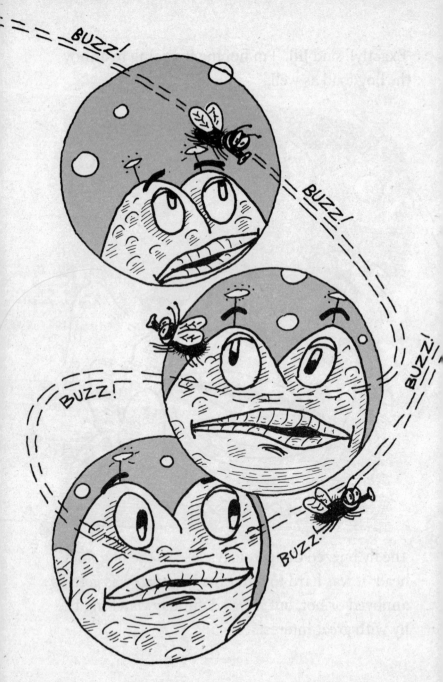

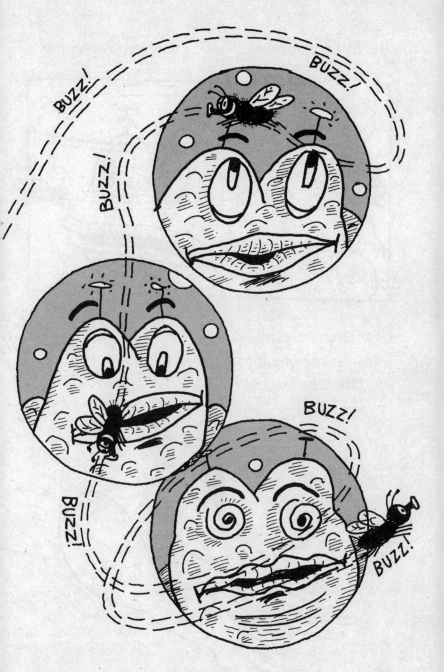

241

The fly kept buzzing. The bog toad kept watching.

Until, suddenly, without warning, the bog toad launched itself into the air and tried to catch the fly.

As the bog toad opened its mouth to swallow
the fly, all the mud that it had sucked up came
gushing out in a great brown wave.

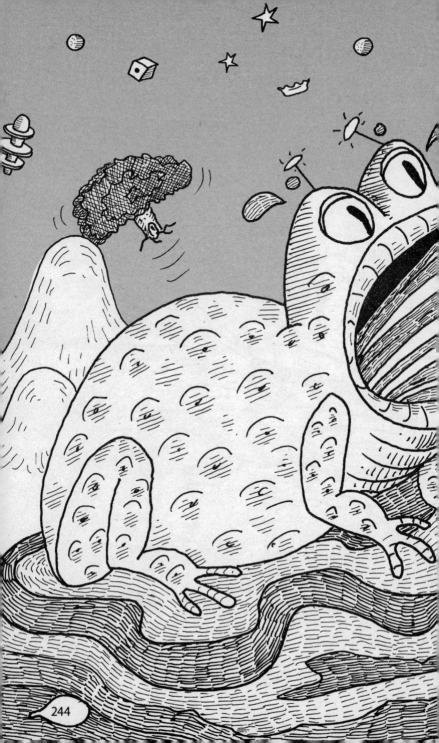

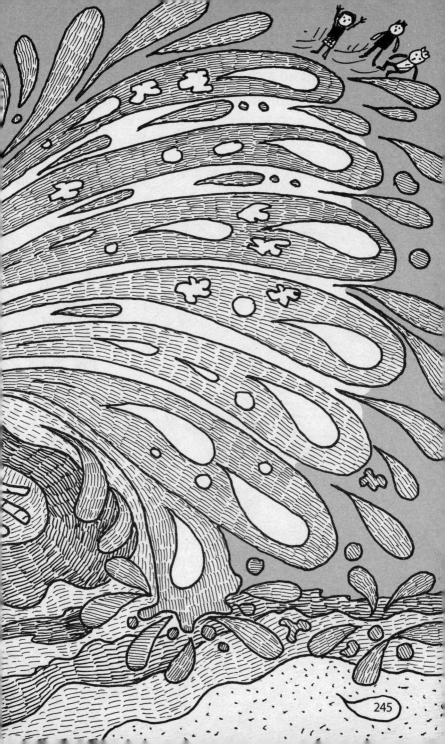

CHAPTER 11

MUD, GLORIOUS MUD!

Actually, when I say 'never to be seen again', what I really mean is 'never to be seen again until we struggled our way back up to the surface'—I was just trying to make it sound more exciting.

We were lost in a vast ocean of mud. For as far as we could see, there was nothing but mud: mud, mud, mud, mud, mud and … more mud.

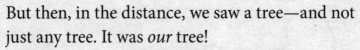

But then, in the distance, we saw a tree—and not just any tree. It was *our* tree!

'There's our tree!' said Terry. 'It's come to save us!'

'Help us!' shouted Jill. 'We're over here!'

We tried to swim towards it, but it was too difficult—the mud was so thick, we could barely move.

'If only we were in the treehouse,' said Terry, 'we could use the GRABINATOR to save ourselves.'

'But if we were in the treehouse we wouldn't *need* to be saved,' I said.

'Oh yeah,' said Terry. 'Good point. Hey, I know! We could use the voice activation option. On the count of three, everybody yell "GRAB"! One, two, three ...'

It worked! One of the GRABINATOR's long arms extended up out of the tree, pulled us out of the mud and dropped us back into the safety of the treehouse.

'Well, we certainly got all the mud out of the bog toad,' said Terry. 'In fact, we got a *lot* more than I expected!'

'We sure did,' I said. 'But where are all the blobs?'

'I don't know,' said Jill. 'It's so hard to see anything in all this mud.'

'Wait,' said Terry. 'I think I can hear them. They're singing. Listen …'

We all leaned out of the tree and put our heads close to the mud, and as we listened we heard the song that the blob had sung when it was telling its story.

'It's the blobs!' I said. 'They're back!'
'Hooray for the blobs!' said Terry.

Suddenly, the blobs stopped singing. At first I thought it was because they were shocked to see us sitting there—they'd probably never seen human beings before—but then I noticed a slurping sound. It was getting louder …

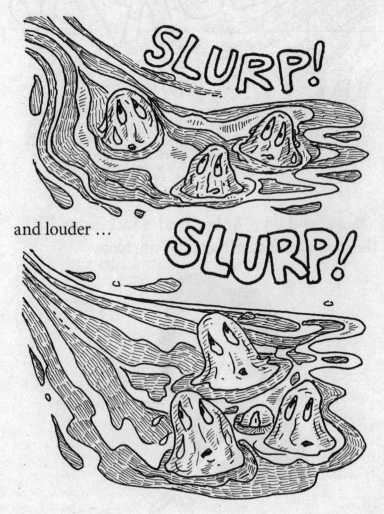

SLURP!

and louder …

SLURP!

and louder.

'Oh no,' said Jill. 'The bog toad is sucking up all the mud again! Watch out, all you blobs!'

Jill needn't have worried, though, because the blobs knew exactly what they had to do to save themselves and they wasted no time doing it.

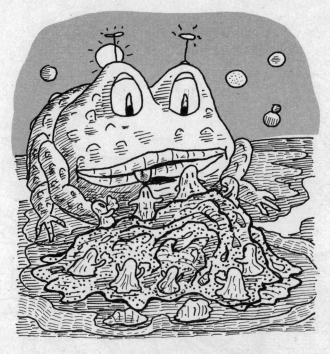

The bog toad immediately stopped sucking up the mud and began licking its lips in anticipation as it watched them.

'They're making it a mud pie!' said Terry.

'Let's help them!' said Jill. 'I love making mud pies!'

'Me too!' I said.

I don't know if you've ever made mud pies, but if you haven't, you should. It's a lot of fun—messy, but fun!

SPLAT!

When the mud pie was finished we all stood back and admired it.

We didn't get to do this for very long, though, because the bog toad immediately started eating it.

It ate …

and ate …

and ate …

until the mud pie was all gone.

The bog toad then let out a big burp,

and hopped away.

The blobs bounced around excitedly.

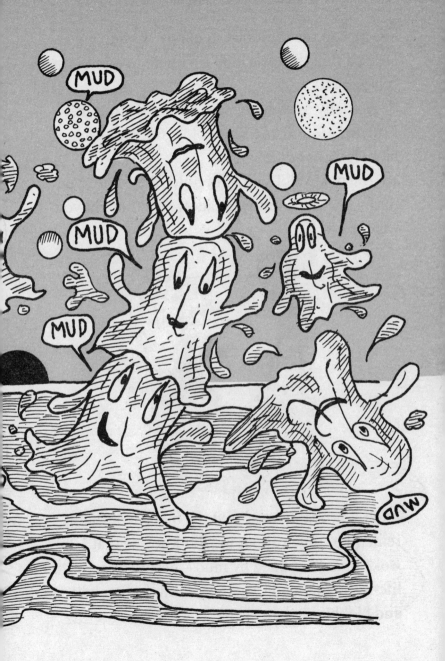

267

'It's nice to see the blobs so happy,' I said, 'but I feel sad that the little blob isn't here to join in the celebrations.'

'Actually, I *am* here,' said a voice behind me. I turned around and saw a blob. But not just any blob. It was *our* blob!

'You're alive!' I said. 'But how? We buried you in the beautiful sunny meadow. We thought you were dead!'

'Well, I probably was,' said the blob. 'Not that I remember much about it. All I know is that I woke up surrounded by mud—beautiful, pure, life-restoring mud! And here I am, feeling better— and blobbier—than ever!'

The other blobs all crowded around.

'I'm sorry I ate the pie and put you all in danger,' said the blob. 'Can you ever forgive me?'

'Of course we can!' said one of the other blobs. 'Everyblobby makes mistakes sometimes!'

It was then that I became aware of an annoying buzzing sound.

'Hey, look,' said Terry. '*Another* fly! What are the chances?'

'That's not *another* fly,' I said. 'It's the exact same one! I'd recognise that annoying buzz anywhere.'

BUZZ!

RETURN OF THE FLY

'But it can't be the same fly,' said Terry. 'It was eaten by the bog toad—we saw it happen.'

'Actually,' said Jill, 'I don't think we did see it happen. We saw the bog toad try to eat the fly but when it opened its mouth, all the mud came gushing out. Maybe the bog toad didn't get a chance to *swallow* the fly.'

The fly buzzed excitedly as if to confirm what Jill was saying. Or it could have just been buzzing because it was a really annoying fly.

'That's the sound we heard just before we were released from the belly of the bog toad!' said one of the blobs. 'Three cheers for the fly!'

'Hooray! Hooray! Hooray!' shouted the blobs. 'Let us sing!'

'Go figure!' I whispered to Terry and Jill. 'On Earth that fly was just an annoying pest, but here on Blobdromeda it's a hero!'

'I'm just glad that the fly—and the blobs—are all okay!' said Jill.

'Well, I guess we should think about getting back home,' I said.

'Can't you stay here with us?' said the blob. 'We could spend our days wallowing and singing in the mud together.'

'That sounds like fun,' I said, 'but we really have to get home and write our next book. We can't write it here—the mud would get all over the paper.'

'I understand,' said the blob. 'There's no place like home. But can we ask a favour before you go?'

'Of course,' I said. 'What is it?'

'Can your fly stay with us? We would honour it as a hero and it would give us great comfort to know it's here—just in case any blobs get swallowed by the bog toad in the future.'

'Are you kidding?' I said. 'That would be more than okay with me!'

'Andy,' said Jill, 'it's not actually your decision to make. It's really up to the fly.'

The blobs turned towards the fly. 'Will you please stay with us forever and ever and ever?' they said. 'Please, please, please?'

BUZZ! BUZZ!

The fly buzzed. It buzzed and buzzed and buzzed and buzzed and buzzed.

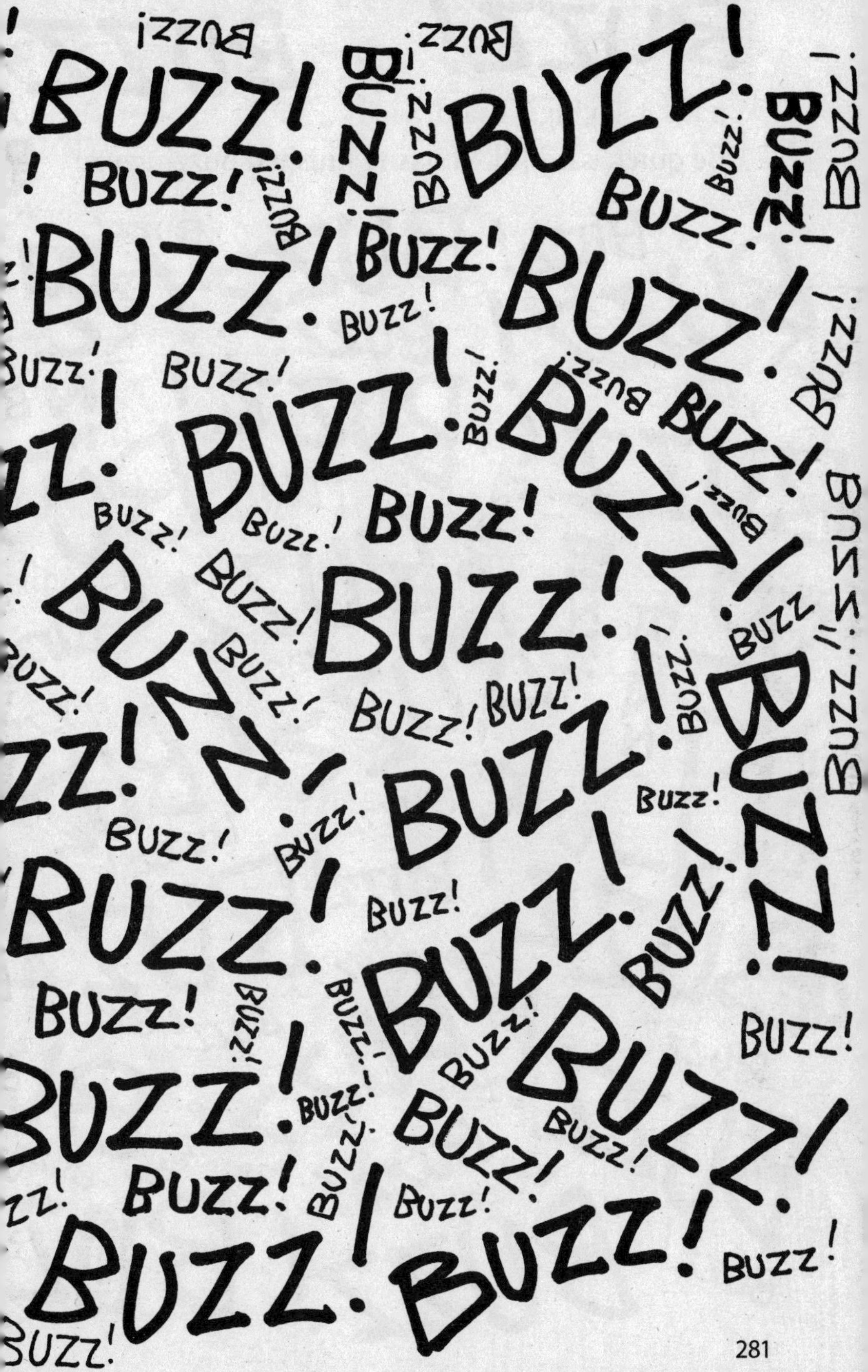
BUZZ!
BUZZ!
BUZZ!
BUZZ!
BUZZ!
BUZZ!
BUZZ!
BUZZ!

BUZZ! BUZZ.

'What's it saying?' I said.

'Be quiet,' said Jill. 'It hasn't finished buzzing yet!'

Finally, incredibly, against all odds, the fly was silent.

'Has it finished now?' I said.

'I think so,' said Jill.

'What did it say?'

'Well,' said Jill, taking a deep breath, 'it said … YES!'

This triggered another celebration and at least another thousand rounds of 'Fly, glorious fly' among the blobs.

'Let's get going,' I said to Terry and Jill. 'Before they realise how annoying that fly is and change their minds about keeping it.'

'Um, there's just one small problem, though,' said Terry. 'Well, when I say "one *small* problem", I mean *three* small problems, and when I say "*three* small problems", I mean three *big* problems: our rocket boosters are all clogged up with mud.'

'Fear not,' said the blob. 'We can super-slingshot you at super-speed back to Earth. You'll be there in no time.'

'Thank you,' I said. 'That would be an amazing help.'

'It's the least we can do after all you've done to help us,' said the blob. 'Get ready for the ride of your life—and hold on tight!'

We climbed back up into the tree … and held on tight.

CHAPTER 13

THE LAST CHAPTER

You wouldn't believe what happened next. I mean,
I wouldn't believe it if I hadn't seen it with my
own eyes.

One group of blobs joined together to form a really big blob with super-strong arms that hugged our tree tight while another group of blobs merged themselves into a giant sling with super-stretchy arms and pulled the tree in the opposite direction.

'Prepare for sling-off,' called the little blob.

The sling-blob pulled and pulled until its arms looked like they were going to snap under the strain.

'Three, two, one … SLING!' shouted the little blob.

BUZZ!

SLING!

The big blob that had been holding onto our tree let go and, with a deafening *TWANG*, we were slung away from Blobdromeda at super-slingshot speed!

Well, that was fun,' said Terry. 'Let's go back to
the time-wasting level and waste some more time.'

'I think we've wasted enough time for one book,' I said. 'And, speaking of which, we've got a book to write—and a *lot* to write about. Let's get started. We should just have enough time to finish it before we get back to Earth.'

And that's exactly what we did.

and we drew …

and we wrote …

and we wrote …

and we wrote …

295

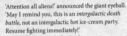

'Attention all aliens!' announced the giant eyeball. 'May I remind you, this is an *intergalactic death battle*, not an intergalactic hot ice-cream party. Resume fighting immediately!'

But the aliens took absolutely no notice—except for one, which looked up at the eyeball and spat hot ice-cream right at it.

It was a direct hit—the hot ice-cream hit the eyeball right in the … well … right in the eyeball!

It went all bloodshot and watery and was obviously in a lot of pain.

That's when I had an idea.

It was possibly one of the greatest ideas I've ever had. Possibly one of the greatest ideas *anybody* has *ever* had in the history of people having great ideas!

142

143

and we drew …

'That's exactly like what happened to us!' said Terry. 'Well, not the bit about the bog toad and the mud and the pie, but *we* were abducted by a giant flying eyeball, too.'

'Those eyeballs sure have a nerve,' said Jill. 'How dare they fly around the universe abducting whoever they like for their horrible intergalactic death battles! I'm *so* glad we got away from them.'

'Don't speak too soon,' I said. 'Look! They're coming after us!'

Uh-oh!

188

189

and we wrote and we drew …

and we drew and we wrote …

and we drew and we drew …

But then, in the distance, we saw a tree—and not just any tree. It was *our* tree!
'There's our tree!' said Terry. 'It's come to save us!'
'Help us!' shouted Jill. 'We're over here!'
We tried to swim towards it, but it was too difficult—the mud was so thick, we could barely move.

250

and we wrote and we wrote …

BUZZ! BUZZ!
The fly buzzed. It buzzed and buzzed and buzzed and buzzed and buzzed.

281

until it was finished and we were almost home!

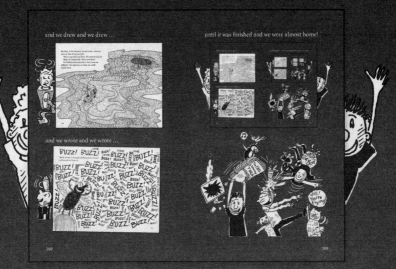

We re-entered our solar system, hurtled towards
Earth …

and landed back down in our forest.

'It's great to be home,' said Terry. 'Let's go for a swim in the see-through swimming pool.'

'Not so fast,' I said. 'We still have to get our book to Mr Big Nose. It's due in FIVE MINUTES!!!'

'Relax, Andy,' said Terry. 'We can just walk over to Mr Big Nose's office and drop it off.'

'I think you're forgetting that Mr Big Nose's office is in the city on the other side of the forest,' I said. 'Even if we *ran* the whole way we'd never make it on time.'

'And I think you're forgetting that we have a super long legs level,' said Terry. 'With our super long legs on, Mr Big Nose's office is just a hop, skip and jump away. Come on!'

We went to the super long legs level where our legs got longer …

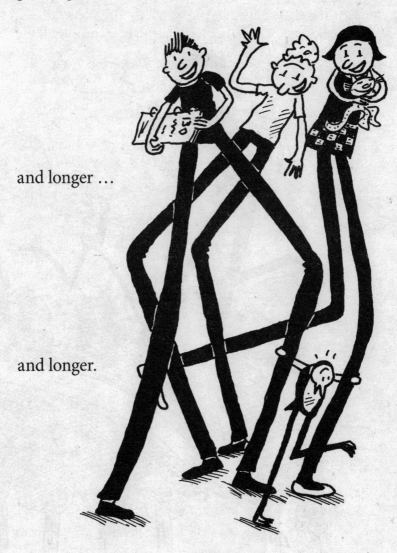

and longer …

and longer.

And then, with a (very long) hop …

a (very big) skip ...

and a (very high) jump …

we reached Mr Big Nose's office and handed our
book to him … right on time!

So, that's the story of how we got abducted by a giant flying eyeball from outer space, fought in an intergalactic death battle, saved all the blobs on Blobdromeda from the belly of a mud-sucking bog toad and got rid of the most annoying fly on Earth. Thanks for reading, have fun and don't forget to keep your eyes on the skies, because you never know what—or who—might be out there!

Lots of laughs

at every level!

Lots of laughs

at every level!

Book →

← Andy

Lots of laughs

at every level!

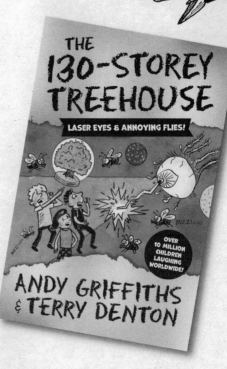

Lots of laughs

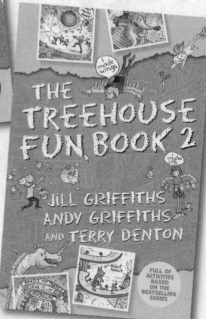

FULL OF ACTIVITIES BASED ON THE BESTSELLING SERIES

at every level!